Sharp Teeth

Ted O'Hare

Bethany, Missouri

Photo Credits:
Cover © Photodisc; Title Page © Susan Flashman; Pages 5, 7, 11 © Corel; Page 6 © Bart Coenders,
Diane Diederich; Pages 9, 13, 20 © Photodisc; Page 12 © Greg Panosian; Page 15 © Beat Glauser; Page 17 ©
Photodisc, Mark Miller; Page 19 © Joe Gough; Page 21 © Clara Natoli; Page 22 © Timothy Craig Lubcke

Cataloging-in-Publication Data

O'Hare, Ted, 1961-
    Sharp teeth / Ted O'Hare. — 1st ed.
    p. cm. — (Animal features)

    Includes bibliographical references and index.
    Summary: Text and photographs showcase teeth
of various animals, from how they are used, to why they
are important.
    ISBN-13: 978-1-4242-1411-2 (lib. bdg. : alk. paper)
    ISBN-10: 1-4242-1411-4 (lib. bdg. : alk. paper)
    ISBN-13: 978-1-4242-1501-0 (pbk. : alk. paper)
    ISBN-10: 1-4242-1501-3 (pbk. : alk. paper)

    1. Teeth—Juvenile literature. 2. Mouth—Juvenile
literature. 3. Animal defenses—Juvenile literature.
[1. Teeth. 2. Mouth. 3. Animal defenses. 4. Animals.]
I. O'Hare, Ted, 1961- II. Title. III. Series.
    QL858.O43 2007
    591.47—dc22

First edition
© 2007 Fitzgerald Books
802 N. 41st Street, P.O. Box 505
Bethany, MO 64424, U.S.A.
Printed in China
Library of Congress Control Number: 2006911277

Table of Contents

What Are Teeth For?

Animals use teeth for many things. They use teeth to find food and to chew it. Animals use their teeth to protect themselves from their enemies.

Many Sets of Teeth

Humans have only two sets of teeth, but some animals have many more. Sharks grow new teeth every two weeks.

Rodents grow new teeth because they **gnaw** away at so many things.

An alligator may have as many as 2,000
ferocious teeth during its lifetime.

Meat Eaters

Animals that eat meat are known as **carnivores**. Their teeth are long and sharp so these animals can gather the food they find. Teeth also help tear the food into pieces that the animals can swallow.

Tigers, wolves, and walruses are all **predators**. At least some of their teeth are sharp.

Meat eaters have **incisors** to bite and cut their food into pieces. They also have canine teeth to stab and kill.

Incisor Teeth

Canine Teeth

Plant Eaters

Animals that eat only plants are known as **herbivores**. Their teeth are flat and wide for easy chewing. Giraffes and horses are herbivores.

Cows are also herbivores. They cut and chew plants.

Elephants are also herbivores. Their teeth can dig up food. They are also used to fight!

Turtles and tortoises do not have any teeth.

Fangs

Fangs

Some snakes have very sharp, hollow teeth known as **fangs**. Some snakes push **venom** through their fangs to kill enemies.

Glossary

carnivores (KAR nuh vorz) — animals that eat meat

fangs (FANGZ) — snakes' teeth, often filled with poison

gnaw (NAW) — to chew or tear

herbivores (ERB uh vorz) — animals that eat plants

incisors (in SY zurz) — teeth used to bite and cut food

predators (PRED uh turz) — animals that hunt and kill other animals for food

venom (VEN um) — poison

Index

FURTHER READING

Perkins, Dorothy. *Let's Look at Animal Teeth.* Pebble Plus, 2006.
Wormell, Christopher. *Teeth, Tails & Tentacles.* Running Press, 2004.

WEBSITES TO VISIT

Because Internet links change so often, Fitzgerald Books has developed an online list of websites related to the subject of this book. This site is updated regularly. Please use this link to access the list: www.fitzgeraldbookslinks.com/af/st

ABOUT THE AUTHOR

Ted O'Hare is an author and editor of children's nonfiction books. Ted has written over fifty children's books over the past decade. Ted has worked for many publishing houses including the Macmillan Children's Book Group.